If you enjoy reading this book, you
might also like to try another story
from the MAMMOTH STORYBOOK series:

Magic Betsey Malorie Blackman

Blair the Winner! Theresa Breslin

Allie's Apples Helen Dunmore

Tricky Tricky Twins Kate Elizabeth Ernest

Pest Friends Pippa Goodhart

Little Mouse Grandma Julia Jarman

First published in Great Britain in 1997
by Mammoth, an imprint of Egmont Children's Books Ltd
239 Kensington High Street, London W8 6SA

Text copyright © 1997 Jenny Nimmo
Illustrations copyright © 1997 David Wynn Millward

The rights of Jenny Nimmo and David Wyn Millward to be identified as the author
and illustrator of this work have been asserted by them in accordance with the
Copyright, Designs and Patents Act 1988

ISBN 0 7497 2751 9

10 9 8 7 6 5 4

A CIP catalogue record for this book
is available from the British Library

Printed in Great Britain by Cox & Wyman Ltd,
Reading, Berkshire

Contents

~

For Nora

J.N. and D.W.M.

1 *Changing Places*

Hot Dog was a large yellowy-coloured dog. No one knew exactly what type of dog he was. He lived with Mr and Mrs Boot who had called him Dennis, after their son, Dennis Boot, who had grown up and left home long ago.

Hot Dog didn't like being called Dennis. It made him think of small fluffy dogs with bad teeth and poor eyesight, whereas he was big, strong, brave-hearted and handsome. In a word, hot. So he called himself Hot Dog.

Mr and Mrs Boot had bought Hot Dog to guard the house. They didn't realise how affectionate he would be. They were kind, but rather old for a big, boisterous dog that wanted rough-and-tumble games and lots of walks in muddy fields and dark, rabbity woods.

Mrs Boot was a tiny, frail old lady. When Hot Dog tried to show how much he loved her, he would rush at her and put his two large paws on her shoulders, and if there wasn't anything handy for Mrs Boot to cling to, over she'd go.

'Dennis!' Mr Boot would shout. 'Don't be so rough! One day Mrs Boot won't be able to get up again.'

Hot Dog would bark to say that he was sorry, but the Boots had to cover their ears because Hot Dog's bark was so loud it made all the china rattle.

Hot Dog's next-door neighbour, Cool Cat, had problems too. His family, the Cranberrys, called him Claude. They thought his name suited a loveable but rather lazy tabby cat. Cool Cat didn't agree. He saw himself as a clever and elegant tom-about-town. In a word, cool. So he called himself Cool Cat.

The two animals were best friends, and every morning they enjoyed meeting at the bottom of Hot Dog's garden to discuss family troubles.

One bright morning Cool Cat appeared on the wall, looking very cross.

'I've had it!' he told Hot Dog. 'I can't stand any more. Luke just tried to take me for a walk.'

Luke was the Cranberrys' son. He was seven years old and very boisterous.

'He never,' said Hot Dog, who knew how much Cool Cat hated exercise.

'He did! He tied some string to my flea-collar while I was asleep, and when I woke up I found myself being tugged outside. Luckily, flea-collars are easy to pull off.'

'I can't believe it. If only it had been me,' Hot Dog said wistfully. 'I'd love to go for a walk with Luke.'

'That's just what I told

4

him, but, of course, he took no notice. I wish I could live with a nice quiet family like the Boots.'

Suddenly, they both had the same brilliant idea. 'Let's swap families,' they said together. 'Right now.'

Hot Dog raced round to the Cranberrys' gate, jumped over it and ran up to the front door. He got his head through the cat-flap but the rest of him was much too big.

Mr Cranberry was fetching the post from the wire basket inside the door.

He didn't see Hot Dog at first and accidentally kicked his nose. Hot Dog let out a howl.

'What are you doing, Dennis?' said Mr Cranberry. 'This isn't your house.'

Hot Dog withdrew his head, ran round to the kitchen window and began to whine.

'What's come over that dog?' said Mrs Cranberry.

'He wants a game!' cried Luke and he ran out into the garden to throw sticks for Hot Dog to chase.

So far so good, thought Hot Dog.

Meanwhile Cool Cat was trying to get into the Boots' house. There was no cat-flap. The Boots just waited for Hot Dog's loud bark and then they would open the door for him. But Cool Cat's miaow was not loud enough. The Boots were both a little bit deaf, although they didn't like to admit it.

'Yowl! Miaow! Yowl!' screeched Cool Cat, pacing the Boots' doorstep. After ten minutes he gave up and went round to the kitchen window. It was too high to reach in one jump, so Cool Cat climbed up the rose trellis until his head popped into view, just above the kitchen sink. Mrs Boot nearly dropped a precious bowl she was drying up. 'Help!' she cried. 'There's a . . . oh, it's only Claude from next door.'

'Miaow!' called Cool Cat wearily.

'What does he want?' said Mr Boot.

'I expect he'd like a nice drop of milk,' said Mrs Boot. 'I don't think the

Cranberrys feed him properly,' and she went to open the door.

Cool Cat lapped up the milk and then he sat on the rug by the stove and began to wash.

'He's got a lovely purr!' said Mr Boot.

'Very comforting!' said Mrs Boot.

So far so good, thought Cool Cat.

'Where's Dennis?' asked Mr Boot.

'Playing with Luke next door,' replied Mrs Boot. 'Can't you hear him barking?'

Mr Boot cocked his head to one side so that he could hear better. 'Best place for that dog,' he said, 'he's too big for us.'

Hot Dog and Cool Cat thought that was that. They'd exchanged families. No more problems. But the Boots and the Cranberrys didn't realise Hot Dog and Cool Cat had planned to swap families *for ever*. That evening Mr Boot carried Cool Cat round to the  Cranberrys' and set him down by his cat-flap. 'Go on, Claude, you live here, not with us!'

Cool Cat hissed. Mr Boot tried to push him through his cat-flap. Cool Cat spat. Mr Boot rang the doorbell and Luke ran to open the door. Hot Dog came chasing after him.

'Here's Claude,' said Mr Boot. 'He's been asleep in our kitchen all day, but now he wants to come home.'

'I don't think he does,' said Luke. 'Not by the way he's clinging to your trousers.'

Mr Boot shook his leg. Cool Cat snarled.

Mr Boot scratched his head. 'Well, I'd better take Dennis home,' he said, 'it's time for his supper.'

'Couldn't he spend the night with me?' Luke begged. 'Mum always says I can have a friend to stay if I want.'

'Well . . .' Mr Boot thought how nice it would be to wake up in a quiet house, without a heavy dog bouncing on his chest and knocking over his tea. And how pleasant it would be to eat breakfast without Dennis snapping playfully at his ankles and rushing off with his slippers. 'How about your parents? Would they agree?'

'You bet! Dad's always saying how he wishes he'd got a dog instead of a cat to keep me company as I'm an only child.'

'I see.' Mr Boot began to feel happy. 'But if Dennis is any trouble just let us know.'

10

'OK. Now you can take Claude back to your place.'

'Thank you, Luke.' Mr Boot picked up Cool Cat and carried him home. Cool Cat's purr was so loud you could hear it two doors away.

Mind you, his problems weren't over. Supper wasn't at all what he expected. Mrs Boot gave him a dog-biscuit. Cool Cat chewed it and spat it out. Mrs Boot tried a spoonful of Dogs' Dinnerkins. Cool Cat licked a chunk and left it.

'Try sardines,' suggested Mr Boot.

So Mrs Boot emptied a tin of sardines on to a clean plate and put it under the kitchen table. Cool Cat's delighted purrs filled the kitchen as he gobbled up every sardine and then licked the plate clean.

Meanwhile, Hot Dog was having trouble too. He couldn't taste the Pusskins Superb and he hated fish. In the end Luke gave him some of his sausages.

At bed-time, Cool Cat's basket was too small for Hot Dog, so Luke made up a bed for him under the kitchen counter. But Hot Dog couldn't sleep. He wanted to be close to Luke to show him how grateful he was for all the games they had played. So, just around midnight, he crept upstairs and jumped on Luke's bed.

Cool Cat wouldn't go near Hot Dog's basket. 'It's dirty!' he miaowed. 'And it smells of dog.'

The Boots didn't understand. They put an old cardigan in a cardboard box and told Cool Cat he would have to spend the night there. Cool Cat

climbed into the box, but, no
matter how much he pressed
and pummelled the cardigan, he
couldn't get comfortable. So, just
around midnight, he crept
up to the Boots' bedroom
and climbed on to the bed
so quietly, so skilfully, that
even though they were light
sleepers, he never woke
them.

When Mrs Boot opened her
eyes the next morning she couldn't
understand what made it so different. 'Of
course, it's the first time in years that I've
woken up with warm feet.' She saw Cool
Cat curled up on the end of the bed and
said, 'I've got a wonderful idea. I wonder
if the Cranberrys would agree?'

Mrs Cranberry was just walking down
to her washing-line when the Boots

appeared at their back door. They almost ran to the fence, both shouting at once.

'Doris, Fred ... please slow down!' said Mrs Cranberry, slightly alarmed at the breathless chatter from two normally quiet old people.

'It's about exchanging Dennis for Claude,' Mr Boot said at last.

'Dennis instead of Claude?' Mrs Cranberry put down her washing-basket. All sorts of pictures began rushing through her head: Luke outside playing with Dennis instead of bouncing footballs down the stairs; Luke taking Dennis for walks instead of practising the drums; Dennis guarding Luke while

she popped down the road to do some extra shopping. 'Let me discuss it with the family,' she said.

The Cranberrys took one minute to make up their minds.

'Yippee!' cried Luke. 'It's not that I don't love Claude, but . . .'

'I said we should have bought a dog all along,' Mr Cranberry reminded them.

It was a very busy day for both families. The Boots fitted a cat-flat. Baskets, brushes and cans of petfood were exchanged, and notes of advice. Last of all, Luke and Mr Cranberry carried Hot Dog's day kennel into their own garden.

That night, just around midnight, Hot
Dog and Cool Cat both crept up the
staircases of their new homes. Hot Dog
jumped on Luke's bed, and Cool Cat
jumped on Mr Boot's and Mrs Boot's
bed. Cool Cat thought, how clever I am
to have chosen such a quiet family and
such a comfortable house. Hot Dog
thought, how lucky I am to have found
a boy who likes being bounced on.

2 The blue blanket

For a few weeks Hot Dog and Cool Cat were very happy in their new homes, and then things began to go wrong.

The Cranberrys had always relied on Cool Cat to keep away the mice. So Mrs Cranberry was quite shocked to see Hot Dog leaping on to the kitchen table when a tiny mouse ran across the room.

'Really, Dennis!' said Mrs Cranberry. 'Do something, for goodness sake!'

Hot Dog whined pitifully.

'You're not afraid of mice, are you?'

17

Mrs Cranberry said. 'It's gone now, you silly dog.'

Hot Dog jumped off the table and ran to the back door.

'All right, you can go and play,' said Mrs Cranberry, 'but I don't want to see any more mice in my kitchen, understand?'

Hot Dog raced to the bottom of the garden, trembling from head to foot, and there he found Cool Cat in a very bad mood. Without waiting to hear his friend's troubles, Hot Dog poured out his own in a whimpering rush.

'I've never heard such rubbish,'

grumbled Cool Cat. 'One tiny mouse and you go to pieces.'

'So, what's eating you?' asked Hot Dog, deeply offended.

'My blanket,' Cool Cat told him. 'Mrs Boot won't clean it.'

'It can't be that bad,' said Hot Dog.

'I'll show you. Follow me!' Cool Cat marched up to the Boots' back door, leaving Hot Dog to scramble over the fence and follow him.

Hot Dog barked and Mrs Boot came to open the door. She was always glad to see Hot Dog.

'Hello, Dennis!' said Mrs Boot, standing well back and holding on tightly to the door, just in case Hot Dog tried to kiss her.

Hot Dog gave a friendly bark and followed Cool Cat into the kitchen. He noticed that it was in a bit of a mess. Mrs

Boot was usually a very tidy person.

'Look!' commanded Cool Cat, staring angrily into his basket. 'Look at that blanket.'

Hot Dog saw a blue woolly blanket with a few tabby hairs on it. 'What's wrong?' he said blankly.

'There are hairs on my blanket,' snarled Cool Cat.

'But they're your hairs,' observed Hot Dog. 'What's wrong with that?'

'They're *old* hairs,' screeched Cool Cat.

Mrs Boot hobbled into the kitchen and said, 'You two aren't quarrelling, are you?'

'No!' barked Hot Dog.

'That's all right then.' Mrs Boot disappeared.

'I didn't know that hairs grew old.' Hot Dog was extremely interested. Cool Cat knew so much more than he did.

'Of course they do,' said Cool Cat, trying to stay calm. 'We lose our hairs all the time. You, me, Mrs Boot, Luke, it happens to everyone.'

'Why aren't we bald, then?' asked Hot Dog.

'Because we grow new ones,' Cool Cat said in a voice that was aching to scream.

'My, oh my!' said Hot Dog. 'New hairs. You mean new hair are being born, right now!'

'Yessss!' hissed Cool Cat.

'How wonderful, just think, new hairs are being born all over me, like puppies.'

'It's not at all like puppies,' screeched Cool Cat. 'Now, what am I going to do about my blanket?'

'You mean you really can't sleep on your own hairs?' asked Hot Dog incredulously.

'Some of them are *six weeks old*!'

'I see.' Hot Dog sat down. 'Have you thought of asking Mrs Boot?'

'Time and time again I've dragged my blanket to the washing-machine. I've even stuffed it inside but she always takes it out and puts it back in my basket.'

'I'll take it to Mrs Cranberry, she'll never notice an extra blanket.'

'Thank you,' said Cool Cat, calmer now. But Hot Dog did nothing except stare at his paws murmuring, 'My, oh my! New hairs are growing!'

'You can't see them growing,' Cool Cat said. Desperately he began to drag the blanket through the cat-flap as quietly as he could. He didn't want Mrs Boot to think he was leaving home. At last Hot Dog helped. He pushed the blanket through the cat-flap and barked to be let out.

'Goodbye Dennis, come again soon,' said Mrs Boot. Hot Dog thought she looked a bit 'down' and hoped she wasn't sickening for something.

Once outside, he dragged the blanket round to the Cranberrys' kitchen window.

'Dennis, what are you doing?' Mrs Cranberry shouted through the open window. 'That's Claude's blanket, take it back at once!'

Hot Dog dropped the blanket and whined. If only Luke was at home.

Just then Cool Cat saw the post van. He raced back home and caught Mrs Boot's letters just as they came tumbling through the letter-box. Carrying them carefully in his mouth, he ran back to the cat-flap. He was just in time to put the two letters on the mat before the postman delivered Mrs Cranberry's mail.

'How strange,' she said, 'how did Mrs Boot's mail get here?' She took it next door. Hot

Dog and Cool Cat followed anxiously.

Mrs Boot was full of smiles. 'This is from the other Dennis,' she cried. 'My son, Dennis, in Australia. Come and have a cuppa with me!'

Hot Dog and Cool Cat followed the two women into the kitchen. Mrs Boot still hadn't tidied up. There were piles of dirty sheets everywhere, and the washing basket was overflowing.

'Excuse the mess,' said Mrs Boot. 'My washing-machine's broken down.'

'I'll do your washing, Doris,' said Mrs Cranberry, 'after we've had tea.'

Hot Dog and Cool Cat hid the blue blanket in the dirty washing. But when Mrs Cranberry went home and began to fill her machine, she found that she couldn't fit everything in. So she left the old blanket for the next wash.

Cool Cat was in despair. To cheer him up, Hot Dog said, 'What about that mouse in our kitchen?'

'Oh, yes.' Cool Cat perked up. 'I thought I'd chased them all out weeks ago. D'you mind if I hang around for a bit?'

'Not at all,' answered Hot Dog.

When Mrs Cranberry left the kitchen, Cool Cat and Hot Dog hid behind the door and waited. Cool Cat's ancestors had survived for thousands of years by keeping quiet at just the right moment. Dogs, however, are different. Hot Dog fidgeted, scratched, coughed, sat down, stood up, turned round and yawned.

'Ssssh!' hissed Cool Cat. 'D'you want me to catch this mouse?'

'Sorry,' Hot Dog apologised. 'I'm just nervous.'

At that moment the tiny mouse scuttled under the table and began to nibble a crumb of toast. Cool Cat tensed his muscles, lowered his head and crept slowly forward, his stomach almost touching the ground. Cool Cat sprang, the mouse fled. They raced out of the kitchen and down the hall.

'Well done, Claude!' cried Mrs Cranberry, opening the back door. 'I knew you'd do it. That dog's useless.'

Hot Dog climbed into his basket. He felt ashamed, humiliated. If only he was as brave and as clever as Cool Cat.

When Luke came home from school he saw Hot Dog's sad face and gave him a big hug.

'Claude caught a mouse this morning,' Mrs Cranberry told Luke.

'Dennis probably feels it was his job,' Luke said.

'Then why didn't *he* catch the mouse?' asked Mrs Cranberry.

'Because dogs don't do that sort of thing,' said Luke.

'What do they do?' asked Mrs Cranberry, irritably.

'They guard people,' Luke told her. 'They rescue people, they play, they have fun, they're companions, they're . . .'

'All right, all right!' Mrs Cranberry gave Hot Dog a pat to show she was sorry.

This gave Hot Dog courage and he dragged Cool Cat's blanket up to her.

'That's Claude's,' said Mrs Cranberry.

'He wants you to wash it,' said Luke. 'You know how Claude hates dirty blankets. Mrs Boot probably doesn't realise. I forgot to tell her.'

'Well, I'm not going to wash it now,' Mrs Cranberry said firmly.

'But Claude won't be able to sleep without it. And he did catch a mouse for you.'

'So he did.' Mrs Cranberry pushed the blanket into the machine for the next load.

Later that afternoon Cool Cat and Hot Dog lay side by side under the Cranberrys' kitchen table. It was very peaceful. Luke was reading his schoolbook, Mrs Cranberry was reading the paper, and Cool Cat was keeping an eye on his blanket as it whirled round in the washing-machine.

'Just look at it,' Cool Cat sighed

contentedly. 'It's a different colour already.'

But Hot Dog couldn't lift his eyes from his paw, where he was certain he could see a new hair just beginning to grow. It was going to be a lovely pale yellow.

3 Cool Cat and the storm

Cool Cat sometimes teased Hot Dog about his fear of mice. Hot Dog thought Cool Cat wasn't afraid of anything, so he couldn't tease him back. Cool Cat kept quiet about the thing he was most afraid of. It made him shiver every time he thought about it. It was called rain, the sort of rain that comes with a storm.

When it rained, Cool Cat usually made quite sure that he kept out of it. If he was in his own garden he just rushed for the cat-flap. If he was down the street he made for the nearest doorway. He knew all the best places for keeping dry. But one day he went far beyond his own street, and it was all because of Mrs Boot's singing.

Mrs Boot loved to sing. She thought she had a wonderful voice. It had become rather quavery and out of tune but she didn't know that.

Mr Boot, being a bit deaf, didn't mind his wife singing, he just turned up the volume on the television so that he couldn't hear her.

Hot Dog had liked Mrs Boot to tra-la round the place, it meant that she was happy, and that made Hot Dog happy too.

Cool Cat *hated* Mrs Boot to sing. It drove him wild. Sometimes he would try to drown her out with his own voice, but today nothing could stop Mrs Boot. She had just heard that the other Dennis was coming home from Australia, with his new wife and baby daughter. Mrs Boot was over the moon. She sang all day, louder and louder.

Cool Cat went to the bottom of the garden but he could still hear Mrs Boot singing. He could even hear her two houses away. He decided to spend the day in another part of town, hoping that she would have lost her voice by the time he came back.

Ignoring the big thunder-clouds that loomed over the houses, Cool Cat set off for the park. He took a short cut across the school playground where Luke and his friend Mark were kicking a ball around.

'Hi, Claude!' called Luke. 'What are you doing here?'

Suddenly there was a deafening crash from the sky. Cool Cat nearly jumped out of his fur.

'Yippee, a storm's coming!' shouted Mark.

Cool Cat raced for the school porch. He got there just in time. The clouds burst and down came the rain.

'Watch out, Claude,' said Luke, rushing into school past Cool Cat. 'You'll be trampled if you stay here.'

Luke was right. Children came pouring off the playground. Cool Cat was surrounded by loud excited voices and big racing feet. He made another dash across the playground and out into the street. The rain came hammering down. Cool Cat was soaked. He ran through the rain, searching desperately for a place to shelter. But the world seemed to have the same idea. There were so many people with wet legs, baskets and push-chairs rushing for cover, and there was no room for Cool Cat in any of the usual places. He became confused and lost his way. And all the time the rain came tumbling down.

At last Cool Cat found a dry place. In a narrow alley someone had conveniently built a little shelter against the wall, to keep the dustbin bags dry.

Cool Cat climbed on
to a bag that seemed
to be flatter than the
rest, and began to groom
himself. He was very muddy.

The thunder continued to
rumble and crash and lightning
streaked across the sky. The rain
settled into a steady downpour and
Cool Cat, exhausted by his dreadful day,
fell fast asleep.

While Cool Cat slept the weather got
worse. The drain beside his shelter was
blocked by leaves and rubbish. The water
couldn't run away and a big puddle
appeared. It grew bigger and bigger. It
swept round Cool Cat's bag and when
he woke up he was surrounded by water.

'Help!' shrieked Cool Cat, leaping out
into the alley. He seemed to be standing
in the middle of a stream. 'Help!' he

screamed again.

Poor Cool Cat really lost his cool.
There were puddles and streams
everywhere he looked. Keeping as close
to the walls as he could, he raced
through the terrifying
wetness until he found
himself in the park. But
the park seemed to be
turning into a lake. The
slides and swings in the
play-area had become
little islands.

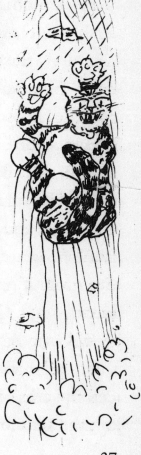

Cool Cat saw one
refuge he could reach.
He ran to the climbing-
frame and clawed his
way to the top. When he
looked down he saw, to
his horror, that water
was now creeping under

the climbing-frame.

'Help!' cried Cool Cat. But there was no one to hear him. The children and their parents had left the park as soon as the storm began.

Back home Mrs Boot was growing anxious. 'Have you seen Claude?' she asked Mr Boot. She had to shout because he still had the television on.

'No,' Mr Boot shouted back. He turned off the television and helped Mrs Boot to search the house. But Cool Cat couldn't be found.

'I'll bet it's the storm,' said Mrs Boot. 'Cats hate storms. Perhaps he's hiding next door. I'll go and ask the Cranberrys if they've seen him.'

When Luke heard that Cool Cat had disappeared he said, 'That's funny. I saw him in the playground and I wondered where he was going. He hates getting wet.'

'Oh dear! I hope he hasn't got lost or . . . or run over. I must find him.' Mrs Boot was almost in tears.

'We'll help you search,' said Luke. 'Dennis will find him.'

Hot Dog barked. He, too, had begun to worry about Cool Cat, and he loved walking in the rain.

Hot Dog led Luke and

the Boots down the street, round the school playground, across the road and down an alley. He found a row of dustbin bags and sniffed them. He smelled bad fish, vinegar, old cans, rotten meat and . . . Cool Cat! He barked excitedly.

'D'you think he's warm?' asked Mrs Boot as if they were on a treasure hunt.

Hot Dog was now leading Luke down the alley, very fast. They reached a wide street and Hot Dog bounded over the zebra crossing.

Wait for us!' cried Mr Boot breathlessly.

'He's going to the park!' called Luke. When he reached the park gates he made Hot Dog wait for Mr and Mrs Boot to catch up, and then they all went into the park together.

They heard a pathetic wailing from the play-area. There were no children on

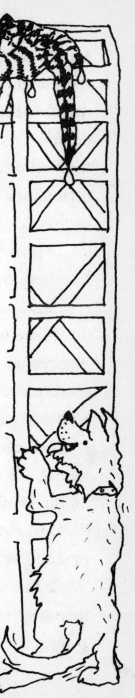

the swings, the slide, the seesaw, or the roundabout, but they saw *something* on the climbing-frame. It looked like a wet rat and it was crying pitifully, 'Help me!'

'Whatever's that?' said Mrs Boot.

Hot Dog knew what it was. He bounded over to the climbing-frame calling, 'Cool Cat, hold on, I'm coming.'

'It's Claude,' said Luke. 'He's so wet his fur is sticking to him.'

'Why doesn't he come down?' asked Mrs Boot.

'He doesn't like water,'

Luke told her.

'But there are only a few puddles left,' said Mr Boot.

'He probably thinks it's a lake,' guessed Luke, and suddenly he saw the funny side of the things and began to giggle. Mr and Mrs Boot joined in.

Above all, Cool Cat hated being laughed at. He turned round until he had his back to them.

Hot Dog sympathised and roared his disapproval. 'Be quiet!' he barked. 'We're all afraid of something. With Cool Cat it seems to be water.'

'I think Dennis is telling us not to laugh,' said Luke. 'Or Claude won't come off the climbing-frame.'

'We didn't mean to laugh, Claude,' pleaded Mrs Boot. 'Please come home. We'll rub you dry and give you your favourite supper.'

Cool Cat wouldn't budge.

'Come on, Cool Cat,' barked Hot Dog. 'You can jump on my back and you won't get your paws wet. But please make sure your claws are in.'

Cool Cat thought about this, then slowly, very slowly, he began to climb down to Hot Dog. When he was one bar away from Hot Dog's furry back he jumped. As Hot Dog carried him safely over to Mrs Boot, Cool Cat hissed, 'Don't you dare mention this, ever again, will you?'

'As long as you promise not to talk about mice,' replied Hot Dog.

'I promise,' Cool Cat muttered quietly.

Mrs Boot swept Cool Cat into her arms and tucked him inside her coat. And, as they all walked home to sit beside a warm fire, and to eat their favourite suppers, Hot Dog and Cool Cat vowed never to mention mice or rain again.

4 *Hot Dog and a catnapping*

In the summer Luke went away with the Cubs. Hot Dog was very lonely without him. Mrs Cranberry kept Luke's bedroom door shut all the time he was away. Hot Dog wasn't even allowed in to sniff over old times.

'You're getting so grouchy,' Cool Cat complained one morning. 'What's wrong with you?'

'I miss Luke,' sighed Hot Dog.

'He'll come back,' Cool Cat told him.

'When?' asked Hot Dog, and a tear formed in a corner of his eye.

'Pull yourself together,' commanded Cool Cat. 'You look a real drag. Your hair's matted and your tail is a disgrace.'

'Luke's not here to clean me up,' whined Hot Dog.

'Suffering shrews!' squealed Cool Cat. 'Who d'you think cleans me up?'

'It's not the same for you,' said Hot Dog. 'You wouldn't like to come for a walk with me, would you, Cool Cat? It's more fun going out with a friend.'

Cool Cat didn't think this was a good idea. 'What about the neighbours? A cat going for a walk with a dog. They'd laugh.'

'Who cares what the neighbours think?' sighed Hot Dog.

Cool Cat was shocked. 'I do,' he said haughtily, and he walked off with his tail held high.

'You're a rotten friend,' Hot Dog called after him. He went indoors and barked at Mrs Cranberry who said, 'I've got to go to work, Dennis. Mr Cranberry will take you for a walk when he gets home.'

Hot Dog knew he would have to wait for hours. He decided to go for a walk by himself.

'Don't go too far,' called Mrs

Cranberry as Hot Dog jumped over the garden wall.

Hot Dog had never been known to wander very far on his own, but today it was different. He felt so lonely he just kept going. He hoped he would find someone to play with, but there was no one about. Nothing was happening. Then, in an unfamiliar tree-lined road, Hot Dog saw something.

Two men in jeans and dirty jackets were creeping towards a small black female cat. 'Here, kitty! Kitty, kitty, kitty!' said one of the men in a high, silly voice. He held out a piece of meat on a stick.

The black cat looked nervous but interested. She took a few paces towards the meat. Hot Dog sat down and watched. The cat and the men drew closer and closer to each other. Suddenly, the cat lunged for the meat, but before she could run off with it, the second man threw a net over her. The cat screamed.

Barking furiously Hot

Dog raced to the rescue. He bit
one man on the bottom
and jumped on the
other one. They
yelled, 'Get off,
you monster!'
and ran to a
blue van parked on
the other side of the
road. Hot Dog chased
them, his joyful barks
resounding down the street.

The men jumped into the van and
drove off, fast, while Hot Dog yapped at
them from the kerb. And then he saw
that the poor cat was still struggling in
the net. Hot Dog ran over and pulled at
the net with his teeth. After a few tugs
the net came free and the little black cat
was gazing up at Hot Dog with wide
yellow eyes. 'Thank you,' she said

breathlessly. 'You saved me.'

'That's OK. Hot Dog at your service. Care for a game?'

'What sort of . . . er . . . game?' asked the cat uneasily.

'You choose,' said Hot Dog generously. 'Running? Chasing? What's your name, by the way?'

'Sadie. Is climbing trees allowed?'

'Naturally.' Hot Dog had forgotten that he couldn't climb trees.

Hot Dog let Sadie have a good start, but his long legs were soon gaining on her. Then she climbed a tree, and that was that. The game seemed to be over.

Hot Dog couldn't even see Sadie's tail as she was so well hidden in the leaves. He barked once or twice but Sadie never replied, so Hot Dog set off for home.

He was just turning a corner into his own street when a white terrier, on the other side of the road, began to laugh at him. 'What's so funny?' called Hot Dog. The terrier wouldn't say.

A Labrador passed by and sniggered, then two dachshunds and the old woman with them began to giggle behind Hot Dog's back. Hot Dog looked over his shoulder and saw that Sadie was following him.

'I think you'd better go home, Sadie,' said Hot Dog. 'People are laughing at me.' At last he knew what Cool Cat meant. It *did* matter what the neighbours thought. Hot Dog began to run. Sadie chased him. This was terrible. It was all wrong. Cats weren't supposed to chase dogs. Suddenly, every garden seemed to have a laughing, sniggering dog or cat leering over the wall. Hot Dog ran faster. He reached his house, jumped over the wall and ran into his kennel. Sadie followed and crept in beside him.

'Look here, Sadie,' panted Hot Dog. 'The game's over. Please go home.'

'I thought I would keep you company for a bit,' she said. 'You've been so kind.'

'It's good of you to say so, but I don't like being laughed at.'

'If we go round the back of your house, we can have a game without anyone seeing us,' suggested Sadie.

This sounded like a good idea. Hot Dog crawled out of his

kennel and, keeping very low, he crept round to the back of the house with Sadie following him. When he was sure nothing and no one could see him he straightened up and whispered, 'Go!'

But Sadie didn't go because there was a shriek from above them. 'Sadie! What are you doing here?' Cool Cat's tabby face peered down from the apple-tree.

'Cool!' squealed Sadie. 'How are you?' And she tore up the tree. They were there for hours, nattering away, and then, when they came down at last, Cool Cat informed Hot Dog that he was seeing Sadie  home. They waltzed off together without looking back, and Hot Dog was left alone again.

'Go off, then. See if I care. You're some friend, Cool Cat,' he called after them.

Mr and Mrs Cranberry got home very late. They forgot Hot Dog's walk. After a while Mr Cranberry got in the car and drove off again.

'That takes the biscuit!' Hot Dog said to himself. 'No one thinks about me. I might just as well not exist.'

He went into his kennel and lay there

feeling very sorry for himself. He was just thinking about asking Cool Cat if he'd like to swop families again, when Mr Cranberry drove up. And out of the car jumped Luke.

Hot Dog dashed down the path just as Luke ran through the gate. 'Dennis, I have missed you so *much*!' cried Luke, hugging Hot Dog.

'Luke, come and have your tea,' called Mrs Cranberry.

'Luke, come and unpack your bag!' called Mr Cranberry.

'Not yet!' said Luke. 'I must have just one game with Dennis. I've bought him a new ball.'

Hot Dog and Luke had the best game

they could ever remember. And afterwards, while Luke was having his tea, Hot Dog lay in the garden, waiting happily for Luke to call him up to bed. Hot Dog had almost forgotten what it felt like to be lonely.

'A-hem,' said a voice beside him. 'Ha-ha! Caught you off guard.' Cool Cat couldn't resist a little dig.

'What d'you want?' asked Hot Dog crossly.

'I've brought you a present.' Cool Cat nosed a large meaty bone towards Hot Dog.

'Where did you . . . ?' began Hot Dog.

'Don't ask,' said Cool Cat. 'It wasn't easy.'

'But why?' Hot Dog was flustered.

'Two reasons,' said Cool Cat. 'You saved Sadie from the catnappers and you're a great guy.'

'Me?' Hot Dog was amazed.

'Yes, you,' said Cool Cat. 'You deserve the best, and I brought you the best because I'm a great guy too, aren't I?'

'Course you are,' said Hot Dog. 'Would you like to share it?'

'Not for me.'

'The neighbours aren't watching.'

'As a matter of fact I don't always pay attention to what the neighbours think,' said Cool Cat. 'You carry on, enjoy it.' He sat beside his friend while Hot Dog gnawed on his bone, and Cool Cat thought how lucky he was to have a good friend, a kind family and, not too far away, a warm, comfortable bed just waiting for him.